THE HIPPO HOP

by
Christine Loomis

illustrated by
Nadine Bernard Westcott

HOUGHTON MIFFLIN COMPANY
BOSTON · NEW YORK 1995

For Susan and Paul,
musically inclined animal lovers

—C. L.

For Becky, Wendy, and Willy

—N. B. W.

Text copyright © 1995 by Christine Loomis
Illustrations copyright © 1995 by Nadine Bernard Westcott

Manufactured in the United States of America

Book design by David Saylor
The text of this book is set in 17.5 point Cooper Medium.
The illustrations are watercolor and ink, reproduced in full color.

HOR 10 9 8 7 6 5 4 3 2 1

Library of Congress Cataloging-in-Publication Data
Loomis, Christine.
The Hippo Hop / by Christine Loomis :
illustrated by Nadine Bernard Westcott.   p. cm.
Summary: A rhyming look at how jungle animals party all night
at the Hippo Hop.   ISBN 0-395-69702-6
[1. Jungle animals—Fiction. 2. Parties—Fiction. 3. Stories in rhyme.]
I. Westcott, Nadine Bernard, ill. II. Title.
PZ8.3.L8619Hi 1995
[E]—dc20   94-31308   CIP   AC

There's a place the animals
Like to go,
Where the palm trees sway
And the breezes blow.

When daylight fades
And the workers stop,
They put on shades
For the Hippo Hop.
They slide,
They glide,
They ride on top,

To the hippening,
Happening Hippo Hop.

Listen to the elephants
Start to wail
On the slide trombone,
Up and down the scale.

The apes play bass and
A crocodile croons
With an all-girl band
Of blue baboons.

They sing,
They wing,
They swing that tune,
At the Hippo Hop
By the light of the moon.

Zebras get jamming
On the ivory keys.
Monkeys bang congas
In the coconut trees.
The sound gets heat
When the tapirs tap.
Snakes keep the beat
While the rhinos rap.

They stay,
They sway,
They play that bop,
And the crowd goes wild
At the Hippo Hop.

Gorilla does splits
On the Hippo Hop floor.
The wildebeest twists
With the brown-eyed boar.
Four lemurs lindy,
An iguana jives,
A mole named Mindy
Gives a frog high-fives.

They dip,
They sip,
They tip the toad,
At the Hippo Hop
Down Soursop Road.

With yaks on sax
The tempo slows.
Giraffes dance closer
In their polka-dot hose.
The baboon girls
Belt "The Beastly Blues,"
And sloths with curls
Slip off their shoes.
They tap,
They snap,
They clap—then stop.

They leave by twos
From the Hippo Hop.

The players pack up
Their horns and snares.
Hippopotami recline in
Green deck chairs.
Capybaras clean,
They shine and mop.
Another night ends
At the Hippo Hop.

They hose,
They close,
They doze, and then

The Hippo Hop
Will open again!

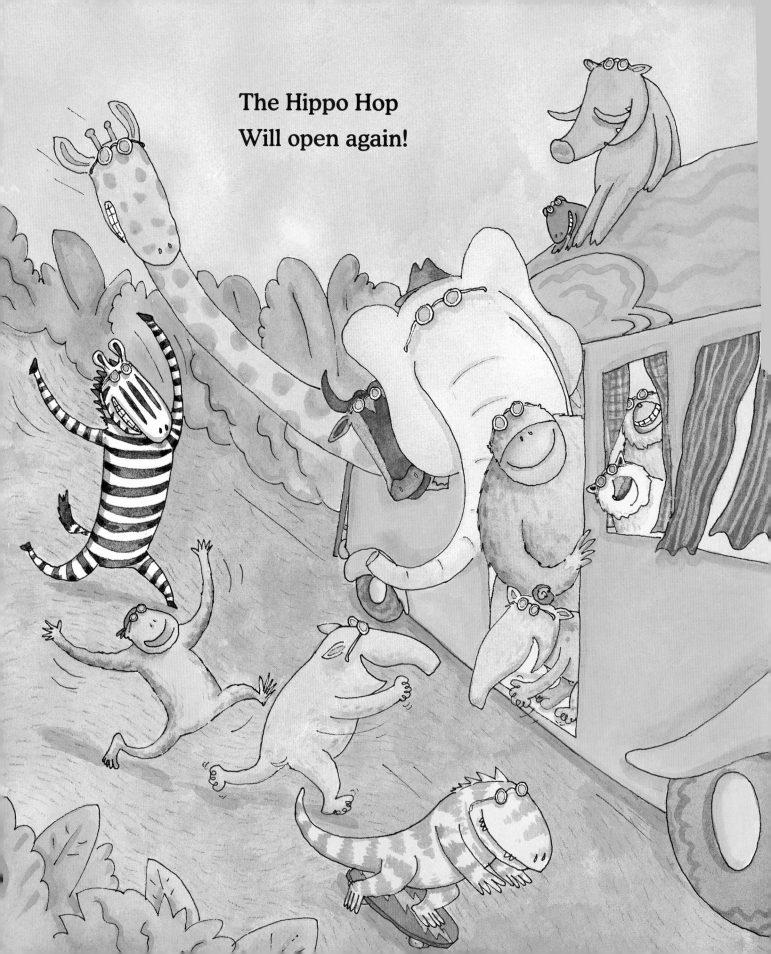